A little girl takes a walk while learning a myriad of new things from her friends. She learns to climb from her friend the monkey. She learns to hide from her friend the rabbit. She learns to watch the night sky from her friend the owl. With simple words and bold illustrations, author-artist Taro Gomi shows children that friends are easy to find even in the most unlikely places—and that you can learn something from everybody.

Al pasearse, una niña aprende con la ayuda de sus amigos un montón de nuevas cosas. De su amigo el mono aprende a trepar. De su amigo el conejo aprende a esconderse. De su amigo el buho aprende a observar el cielo nocturno. Con palabras sencillas e ilustraciones acentuadas, autor y artista Taro Gomi demuestra a los niños lo fácil que es encontrar amigos aún en los lugares más inesperados—y que se puede aprender algo de cada uno.

"A little girl recites all the pleasurable things she has learned from her friends . . . including such meaningful things as reading and studying and, most importantly, loving . . . An elemental story that will reach toddlers and older preschoolers alike." —*Booklist*

"The illustrations are vibrant. The story is simple . . . Children will quickly be pointing out the whimsical details in the art." —*Parents' Choice*

"Una niñita relata todas las lecciones gratas que le han enseñado sus amigos . . . incluyendo las cosas significantes como leer y estudiar, y más importante, amar . . . Un cuento elemental que conmoverá tanto a los más pequeñitos como a los más grandes de edad preescolar." —*Booklist*

"Las ilustraciones son vibrantes. El cuento es sencillo . . . Los niños se divertirán señalando los detalles originales de los dibujos." —*Parents' Choice*

First bilingual English/Spanish edition published in 2006 by Chronicle Books LLC.

Copyright © 1989 by Taro Gomi.

English text copyright © 1990 by Chronicle Books LLC.

Spanish text copyright © 2006 by Chronicle Books LLC.

All rights reserved.

First published in Japan by Ehonkan Publishers, Tokyo.

English translation rights arranged through Japan Foreign Rights Centre.

Book design by Anne Ngan Nguyen.

Typeset in Futura.

Manufactured in China.

Library of Congress Cataloging-in-Publication Data

    Gomi, Taro.

        [Minna ga oshiete kuremashita. English & Spanish]

        My friends=Mis amigos / Taro Gomi. — 1st bilingual English/Spanish ed.

          p. cm.

        Summary: A little girl learns to walk, climb, and study the earth with help from her friends, most of which are animals.

        ISBN-13: 978-0-8118-4849-7 (library ed.)

        ISBN-10: 0-8118-4849-3 (library ed.)

        ISBN-13: 978-0-8118-5204-3 (pbk.)

        ISBN-10: 0-8118-5204-0 (pbk.)

        [1. Growth—Fiction. 2. Animals—Fiction. 3. Spanish language materials—Bilingual.] I. Title. II. Title: Mis amigos.

        PZ73.G587 2006

        [E]—dc22

        2004017115

Distributed in Canada by Raincoast Books, 9050 Shaughnessy Street, Vancouver, British Columbia V6P 6E5

10 9 8 7 6 5 4 3 2 1

Chronicle Books LLC, 85 Second Street, San Francisco, California 94105

www.chroniclekids.com

MY FRIENDS
MIS AMIGOS

by Taro Gomi

chronicle books · san francisco

I learned to walk from
my friend the cat.

De mi amigo el gato aprendí a caminar.

I learned to jump from
my friend the dog.

De mi amigo el perro
aprendí a brincar.

I learned to climb
from my friend
the monkey.

De mi amigo el mono aprendí a trepar.

I learned to run from my friend the horse.

De mi amigo el caballo
aprendí a correr.

I learned to march from my friend
the rooster.

De mi amigo el gallo
aprendí a marchar.

I learned to nap from my friend the crocodile.
De mi amigo el cocodrilo aprendí a echar una siesta.

I learned to smell the flowers
from my friend the butterfly.

De mi amiga la mariposa
aprendí a oler las flores.

I learned to hide from my friend the rabbit.

De mi amigo el conejo aprendí a esconderme.

I learned to explore the earth from my friend the ant.

De mi amiga la hormiga aprendí
a explorar la tierra.

I learned to kick from my friend the gorilla.

De mi amigo el gorila aprendí a patear.

I learned to watch the night sky
from my friend the owl.

De mi amigo el buho aprendí a
observar el cielo nocturno.

I learned to sing from my friends
the birds.

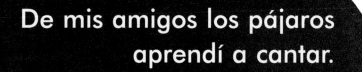

De mis amigos los pájaros
aprendí a cantar.

I learned to read from my friends the books.

De mis amigos los libros aprendí a leer.

I learned to study from my friends the teachers.

De mis amigos los maestros aprendí a estudiar.

I learned to play from my friends
at school.

De mis amigos en la escuela
aprendí a jugar.

And I learned to love from a friend like you.

Y aprendí cómo amar de un amigo como tú.

Taro Gomi attended the Kuwasawa Design School in Tokyo. He has illustrated more than three hundred books for children, garnering him many awards. Mr. Gomi now lives in Tokyo, Japan.

Taro Gomi asistió a la escuela de diseño Kuwasawa en Tokyo. Ha ilustrado más de 300 libros infantiles, por lo cual lo han premiado mucho. Sr. Gomi vive ahora en Tokyo, Japan.